MILDEW

Paulette Jonguitud is a Mexican author who has written two novels and a children's book. She is now working on a theatre play.

PAULETTE JONGUITUD

Mildew

translated from the Spanish by the author

CB editions

The author is grateful to Claudio Lafarga, Beverley Bie Brahic and the MacDowell Colony.

First published in the UK in 2015
by CB editions
146 Percy Road London W12 9QL
www.cbeditions.com

Originally published in Spanish as *Moho*
in 2010 by Conaculta, Mexico

Printed in England by Blissetts, London W3 8DH

ISBN 978-1-909585-03-4

MILDEW

Never forgive, I said that morning just as I do every morning, by the window, waiting for dawn. Never forgive. Whom? Constanza? Which one of them? Never forgive her, the young Constanza, or myself, the old one? I did not know, all I knew was: I was never to forgive.

'It hasn't been that long, mother, it's normal if you feel lonely,' my daughter Agustina had said a few days before. I don't feel lonely, it's this house that suddenly has an echo.

The dark sky was melted with the fence, the tree, the houses of the neighbourhood. Things were not yet solid. There, out of focus, I could be young again, my flesh could be firm, I could imagine the house full of family, I could imagine my children, Leonel and Agustina, asleep in their beds.

Once the house was always full of people but now it was an exhausted shell, restless before dawn, a deep silence barely disturbed by the dogs barking. The dogs, the only crew members that hadn't jumped ship.

In darkness everything is the same, everything is safe. Later: who knows. The sun comes up, the city grows noisy, the shadows are just imitations of form. Darkness was beginning to crack. With light comes reality. It was the start of a day of false calm, or that's what I thought: twenty-four hours for the house to sleep before it opened its doors to an army of workers with tents, tables, dance floor: Agustina's wedding.

When the sky grows orange, colour invades every object and transforms it, the curtains catch fire and the grass tries to shimmer as much as the sky does. I don't like dawn. I said goodbye to darkness the way one does when leaving a shelter to walk in the rain.

I went into the bathroom and undressed in front of the mirror. I did not find in my reflection the young woman I had been just seconds ago. I examined my body, a personal audition that I fail every morning. Big feet, varicose ankles, wide thighs.

A slight prickling in the pubis made me look down and I found a green spot, half hidden by pubic hair. It looked like a mole, irregular in form and velvety to the touch. It seemed to be covered by grey powder. I scratched but it did not go away. If anything the spot looked even larger.

I went into the shower, under very hot water. I scratched, I rubbed, I scraped: the spot was still there. I tried every cleaning product I could find, pouring them over myself. Nothing changed. Then I attacked the spot with a metal nail file: the skin got irritated but the spot was undisturbed. I cut myself with the tip of the file. The blood looked black over the green spot.

I covered the wound with a cotton ball. I don't like surprises and since the last one had been an affair between my husband and my niece, I was not feeling in the mood for another one.

Six months earlier I had designed the costumes for a production of *Macbeth* and there, in the bathroom, all the bad omens came to my mind and for a moment I convinced myself that I had been struck by a curse: *Out, damned spot! out I say!*

When the bleeding stopped I removed the cotton ball to find that the green mole had grown towards the leg. It was getting wider and solid. I examined it carefully: it was dark in the centre, olive green, and its edges were lighter. I separated the skin where I had cut myself and saw that the green went down and into the flesh.

Do not cry.

The spot got wider and wider, it grew before my eyes, it developed white filaments like a dandelion. When I moved my leg the filaments swayed: fragile tips, firm roots, like a miniature field. I wet my finger with the tip of my tongue and ran it over the spot, then I licked it again: the mole felt like flour and had no taste.

I still smelled of cleaning products and alcohol but the voice of my mother rang through the empty bathroom: *Look how dirty you are!* My mother from before, the one who was not yet a widow, my once useless mother who was incapable of ironing a shirt, the one who knew how to cook only beef stew and flour tortillas. That mother who used to walk around the house as if she were asleep and who only came alive to say: clean your shoes, fix your braids.

When my father was still alive my mother did nothing around the house, she only cared for herself. She never asked if the children had eaten, if we had done our homework. We had other people for that. *Look how dirty you are!* My sister Nilda used to escape through the back door and hide in a neighbouring orchard just to see how long it took mother to notice she had gone, but Nilda always came home, starved and angry, before anyone had noticed her absence. I don't like to think about my mother like that, combing her hair in front of a mirror without a thought for her nine children. Nine. I have only two and they drive me insane. Three. Do I have three children? No. Two. Only two that count.

I don't like to remember that decorative mother. I prefer to think of her as she was when I found her after the funeral: physical, real. She was functional and ashamed for not knowing how to handle my father's inheritance. She soon lost everything in bad investments. She lost the shoe factory which had taken my father a lifetime to build, she lost our house, she lost it all. I have always tried not to see her as a failure and I prefer to look at her strong sons instead, at her useful daughters trained not to repeat her mistakes.

Oh, mother, if only you could see me now.

My father had a stroke when I was nine years old. We lived in Chihuahua, in a house that I found enormous even though it was only a one-storey building. My brother Tavo and I were the youngest of nine and when my father got sick we soon became a nuisance, like old furniture that always gets in the way. Tavo was a small and skinny boy with spiky hair and large front teeth. I think I was the only one who loved him, at least I was the only one who took care of him. 'Did you eat?' I used to ask him and his answer was always 'No' so I took him to the kitchen and fed him bean burritos. Maybe that is why today he is still a child, a forty-five-year-old child who spends the day in his workshop, buried in machinery, with that fanatical attention to detail that only autistic children seem to have. When my father got sick some of the machines from the factory were brought to the house, where they soon occupied the garage. Tavo spent a long time playing with them. Today it is hard to catch him without grease on his fingers, without a screwdriver in his pocket.

I have a lot of memories of my father but of one of those memories, the crucial one, I am uncertain. If I don't think about it that much I know that I saw him that day, the day he had the stroke, I know I did. But then I doubt it. My father was always the first to wake up and he walked through the house, singing loudly, to wake everyone else. It seemed to me that he had a different song for every day of the year. We started our day to the sound of his footsteps and the sound of his voice. In this memory it is early in the morning and I hear my father's footsteps, I open my bedroom door and I see him walking by: his eyes seem sunken, a hand on his chest, the hat about to fall from his head. He looks at me. Maybe he wants me to help him. No, it is a fact, he is asking for my help. I look down at my bare feet, my nightgown, and I close the door. A doubtful memory. The next time I saw him he was lying in bed.

When my dad got worse, when he could sing only one verse of a single song, when he could not recognise his own hands and woke up startled by the sound of his own breath, my mother came to me and said: 'You will be going to a new school.' I was delighted: new uniform, new shoes, even new underwear. My sister Flor was also coming and we got in the car together, happy to leave behind a house where we could no longer play: *shh, Dad is sleeping*. The school was in an ancient hacienda building and I loved its great stone walls, its quince trees. It had a garden where large tomatoes grew, overlooked by a set of swings I promised myself I would spend hours on every day. The dark hallways were cold and the yard seemed endless. A nun showed us the dormitories and I assumed they were for the staff. That first day went very fast among a whirlwind of nuns' habits, girls' shouting and the promise of an escape into the pantry. But the day became afternoon and then night and no one came to pick us up. We spent two years in that boarding school.

I never knew who packed my bag to take me there, who embroidered my name on the new uniforms, who forgot to pack the doll with a sucker. Had anyone told Tavo that we would no longer play in the bathtub, that we would no longer tell stories to one another through the garden hose? I never knew who forgot to pack my toy tea set. No dolls, no story books, no box of memories. Everything was left behind. I had only my fear.

When I was finally happy at boarding school a nun dragged me out of class and two hours later I found myself, dressed in black, standing in line with my eight brothers and sisters by my father's coffin. 'Who is in that box?' asked Tavo. I didn't answer. Maybe I was not sure.

My mother, my sister Flor, Tavo and myself left Chihuahua shortly after the funeral. We had lost the factory, the house, Chihuahua. My first train ride was bitter. We got to Mexico City and found an apartment with no quince trees, no garden, nothing.

The prickling in my thigh kept growing stronger and the spot looked bigger. I looked around the bathroom: the shower, the curtain, the dark stain under the pipes from which water dripped to the floor. I lost my breath for a second and then rushed to that dark stain on the tiles. It was an exact replica of the spot that grew on my leg. I compared them slowly: tile, leg: identical. It was the same green, the same vegetation. Twin spots.

Mildew.

Was that even possible? Of course not, you have lost your mind. No, I am not insane, I am angry, that must be it. That healthy anger that makes you strong. That had to be it. After all, this mess between Felipe and Constanza had to affect me somehow, right? That had to be it, the arsehole in love with Constanza, the young one. The man who sings songs to her over the phone, who writes poems and dreams of taking her out to dinner. Pathetic.

I always wanted a man who was like my father, at least as I remembered him: a big man with a deep voice and hair on the back of the hands. Felipe was nothing like him and I won't deny that for years I held against him the fact that he could not fill my father's shoes. A father with whom

I lived for less than ten years. A father I had made up from a patchwork of memories.

I licked the mildew on the floor – same feeling, velvety and tasteless. Shit. I should at least call a doctor. But I felt like lying on the floor and shouting: How dare you, in my own house? Do not cry. Was I crying for her? For him? So far these wounds seemed not to hurt me. It made me sick to think that someone could feel sorry for me: Poor Constanza, did you hear what they did to her?

I had to work on a plan of action. I was not going to spend all day locked in the bathroom with Agustina's wedding hanging over my head. Twenty-four hours to reconstruct myself, not a minute longer. First: I had to learn as much as I could about the invader. Mildew. The name was a start, a possibility.

Naked, I left the bathroom. The sun had already set every corner of the house on fire.

It was raining when I found out about Felipe and my niece. But was it, really? I remember the sound of the water on the roof, but I am not sure, it might just be a touch of nostalgia. I like the rain and I would have loved to be surrounded by it at such a time. So: it was raining.

It was after ten that night. I walked in silence through the dining room, I assumed everyone was upstairs. And then I found Felipe and Constanza sitting at the table, their heads close together as though they were sharing a secret, a bottle of wine between them. I did not need to see much more. Those few seconds were enough for me to know that I didn't belong there. The furniture seemed to know I was there and feel ashamed, I heard the table creak and saw the chairs wanting to tip over to one side. The edge of the wine glasses, my glasses, seemed to shrink when touched by those lips.

When Felipe finally looked up it was quite clear to everyone: we all knew what was going on. It is not necessary to find two people in bed, one just has to look carefully at the way they touch the edge of a glass, how they caress a bottle with their fingers. And even though something was breaking, there was no shouting, no tears, no one pulled at their hair or looked at the sky with an open mouth, no one broke plates or dragged suitcases to the front door.

I whispered 'Sorry', and went upstairs to the bathroom. Constanza followed me. I tried to think of her as the little girl I had brought up: round nose, messy curls. But I could not find that girl in the woman standing next to me: thirty-eight years old, green blouse with a deep neckline that showed off her large breasts, curls dyed the exact same red as mine. She smiled. Was she laughing at me?

When did you get so big, Constanza?

I had to admit it: Felipe was not a pervert and Constanza was no longer a little girl. Too bad. I would have loved to hear her cry. I would have loved to say to Felipe: You are a pig! But he wasn't. Not really. She had opened the doors willingly and that was what she was letting me know right there, in silence: I won, and you didn't even notice we were in a battle.

Shit.

We removed our make-up in silence. The eyes got undefined, the mouths got pale, the under-eye circles became darker. Once exposed we could no longer stay in silence. She spoke first and told me that Felipe had picked her up from the airport and that she had cooked dinner to thank him.

'He kept talking about you,' she said. 'All complaints, you know?'

Under the pretence of taking a shower she began to undress. I kept quiet in order to choose my words carefully, I didn't want to be caught by surprise again. She took off her bra and her heavy breasts fell a few centimetres. Was she moving slowly? I remember her as in slow motion. I felt that she inhabited every last corner of her body, she commanded it, she was alive in every toenail, every inch of her knees, even her earlobes. She liked her body, she lived in it as owner and not as a guest. I envied her.

'You know him, he kept saying he felt like a guest in his own house,' she said.

I looked at her dark nipples, large as ancient coins, and I remembered that those breasts had fed two children. We were alike in that respect. But I was not an ungrateful bastard who bites the hand that once fed her. Didn't that have to count for something? It did not.

'Why are you here?' I asked.

Constanza was almost an orphan. My sister Flor got pregnant when she was very young and there was no way for her to take care of a baby so she took her daughter to my mother's house. I still lived there. Flor was like that: beautiful and irresponsible. At first Constanza was like a little sister to me, someone to keep me busy when I got back from school. She spent the first five years of her life with us and she didn't seem to know who her real mother was. I think she chose me because we shared the same name.

'I'm here to work,' she said. 'They sent me to spend some time in the Mexico office. I was glad, to tell you the truth, it's been ages since I last came to visit. The house looks just the same. Are you listening to me?' she asked and removed her pants.

She wanted my eyes on her body, she was removing her clothes to show me the ground where she had won the battle I didn't know we were fighting.

'I am telling you, Felipe is feeling very lonely,' she said. 'I would be careful if I were you, he might seek company elsewhere.'

She was threatening me. She dared to threaten me, the little bitch. Who do you think you are talking to? Who scraped you off the floor of so many shitty bars? Who found the clinic to get rid of your first child? Lucky him, I have always thought, lucky him that he never came, he never met you, lucky him that he went back to wherever he came from. Away from you. I said nothing. Oh well, I still had some pride left, I still had some of my old haughtiness: this is not happening to me.

'How are your kids?' I asked so we didn't have to talk about Felipe.

'They are fine, with their father. I needed a break. These few weeks here with my family will be perfect for me,' she said.

I could see scars on her hands and I remembered that afternoon when I came back from school and couldn't find her. I checked the closets, behind the curtains, and I finally found her under the dining table. When I moved the tablecloth she was sitting there with her hands covered in blood, a knife by her side. 'What the hell are you doing?' I said, pulling her out of there. 'Nothing! I'm only playing,' she answered.

She removed her underwear and picked it up with her

foot. I couldn't stop myself from looking at her shaved pubis. I pictured her walking naked around my house, her arse reflected in the polished wood, her thighs resting against the windows.

When she turned six Constanza went back to her mother, who was pregnant again. Flor had decided to start a *proper family.* Constanza left kicking and screaming: 'Why do you let her take me away?' she yelled at me from the back of the car. The *proper family* never really worked out and Constanza developed the anger of those who are orphans everywhere they go. Her time with her mother was thunderous and she never got along with her brothers and sisters. One day she threw herself down the skylight and her mother decided she had had enough. Constanza came back to me with both arms in casts, seven suitcases and a poorly disguised smile on her face. 'You are much more her mother than I am,' said my sister and she left. But I was married and had two children of my own by that time. I don't think Constanza liked the company very much but she had to get used to it and within a couple of years I thought I had finally domesticated her.

Naked, I went upstairs to my studio and when I opened the door the first thing I saw was the fake chandelier we had used for *Macbeth* and that now hung over my working table, over the shelves covered in different fabrics, the mannequins, the photographs and posters of all the shows I had worked on during two decades as a costume designer.

It was there, in my studio, where everything had started. Among my sewing machines, my baskets full of thread, my sketches, my books.

I walked across the room to look at Agustina's wedding gown that hung on a dress form. It seemed to belong to a different time, a different life. I still had to sew the ruffles of the skirt, do the hem, braid the straps for the corset. Twenty hours to go, twenty hours which I had planned to spend sewing, alone in my studio, listening to a Joan Manuel Serrat record, safe and happy with my pins and needles and the hypnotic *clac clac clac* of the sewing machine that I found so comforting.

I had planned. Before. When? I walked across the room without looking at the mirrors that still contained the image of Constanza trying on dresses, lifting her skirt, lowering her neckline, and Felipe behind her whispering the same word over and over again: 'Shorter.'

I had fallen into that trap once before. I had stopped and looked into the mirrors and heard what they had to say. When Felipe told me about him and Constanza I went upstairs to hide in my studio, to let my body cool down, to look for a place to store the rage that overwhelmed me so that I wouldn't end up like my father, lying in bed after a stroke, whispering the same line of the same song over and over again, incapable of going to the bathroom by himself. But once I got to my studio the mirrors became pictures in which I saw my niece, all smiles, and my husband behind her. What happened here? The reflection of Constanza laughed and told me what I already knew: she was there to pick up a dress that I had made for her but when she got to the studio she decided to try on a few other dresses and Felipe offered to help her choose. They were alone. She tried on a couple of dresses while Felipe watched her, sitting by the mannequins. 'Sitting right here,' said Felipe's reflection in the mirror, sweaty palms and all. And Constanza's reflection told me that she kept lifting her dress and asking: 'Should I make it shorter?'

Not today. There were still traces of ungiven kisses hanging from the ceiling and I walked through them as if they were a spider's web, thin strands tangled with my hair. *Look how dirty you are!* I walked on my tip-toes, bare feet on the wooden floor that suddenly felt dirty, and I reached the desk and the computer. I sat there, turning my back on the room and on Constanza watching me from the mirror, lifting her dress and showing her underwear. Shorter. Shorter.

Mildew. Concentrate.

I never imagined such variety. I read, I compared, I took notes and did sketches until I found, for the third time that morning, the now intimate vegetation. The technical information said: *cladosporium*. Or something like that. I forget. But could this grow on human skin? I searched for a webpage that listed skin diseases and started browsing the images. Black spots consumed an old man's legs. Some sort of fungi devoured a man's arm and transformed it into something I can only describe as a tree branch.

Shortly after I got to boarding school I stole a book. I wanted to read *The Wonders of the Animal Kingdom* – the nuns had banned it from the library because it showed animals copulating. When the librarian was looking the other way I snatched the book and hid it under my blouse and then ran to my dormitory, where I discovered that I had taken the wrong book. This one was red and had an owl on the cover. It said BOSCH in white letters. I opened it and found three gardens in one picture. I got lost in them. I figured it was a children's book because it was full of drawings of animals and strange beasts: two birds fought over a lizard, a mermaid with the face of a duck read a book in a pond. In the first garden there was a man who looked a lot like Jesus. It made me laugh because he was wearing a pink tunic. I looked at the silver cross nailed to the door of the dormitory and knew that if I asked the nuns why Jesus was wearing a pink dress they would answer: the Lord can wear whatever he wants to. I rubbed my thighs together, my eyes glued to those pictures of bodies riding pigs and donkeys. I looked carefully at every naked body and put my fingers between my legs. Then I reached the third garden, the third picture: black sky, broken bodies. That had to be the place where the nuns said bad girls ended up, those girls who exchanged kisses under the sheets, those girls who stole wine from the chapel. One image stuck with me in my nightmares for years: a man cut in half with ants living inside him, ants sitting at a table.

I hadn't thought about those images in nearly forty years; I had nearly forgotten that sweaty night in which I convinced myself that the heat I felt was that of hell coming closer and closer. But while I looked at all the different skin diseases, my heart raced just like it had done back then. It was a freak show, photo after photo, skin after skin. The scientific names meant nothing to me: *ichthyosis, granulosis, erythroderma.* I held on tight to my desk, afraid that I would drown among those wilting skins in a sea of legs with rashes, of babies wrapped in bloody membranes.

One image in particular scared me so much that I couldn't stop looking at it. It was a small baby inside an incubator, his eyes closed by something that looked like seashells. What had its mother felt when she pushed it out of her womb? Relief? But don't all mothers feel relief?

Then I found the picture of a boy covered in scales. He looked as if he had been submerged in mud and then put out in the sun to dry, and through the mud that had cracked I could see thin lines of healthy skin. My feet felt cold. The freak was looking directly at me: a goblin, a baby dragon, long eyes, hair sticking out at the back of his head, face covered in earthy scales. Scales. Green. Like my spot. Like me. Had his transformation begun slowly, like mine? Or maybe he just woke up one morning to find that he had turned into – what? He was no longer a boy, he was something else. Would I stop being a woman? Would my body decompose? Would my limbs fall off?

Not one damned answer. Only mildew. *Cladiosporum*. Green. I was afraid even to move my head, I didn't want to find Constanza making fun of me from the mirror. The boy-crocodile kept looking at me, beyond human, beyond disgust. I imagined my picture right next to his. What would be written in the caption? A *nahual*? A basilisk? What would I become? I laughed. Or I think I did. I would have liked to laugh.

The boy was welcoming me to the bestiary. Don't look at me. Where could he be at that precise moment? Locked up in a lab somewhere? Touring with a circus? The goblin boy, the boy-crocodile. The woman-what?

Move, close the picture, navigate away from that page, turn the computer off. Under that boy's gaze my body refused to obey. I closed my eyes but he was already inside me, inside my eyelids: 'I'll stay here to keep you company,' he said.

'Get out!'

The boy-crocodile discovered my spot and jumped up and down, happy. 'That makes two of us, I knew I couldn't be the only one,' he said. 'No. No. No. We are nothing together. There is no *we*.' I opened my eyes to find him trapped inside the computer screen again. I preferred to see him that way, horrible but distant. Go away, lizard-boy. I don't have scales, my eyes are not yellow, I don't need compassion.

I threw up under the table, on a few discarded sketches. And then I saw that the mildew had reached my knee.

Come on, move! And then I did move and my hand jumped and closed the photograph on the screen and I let my legs carry me to one of the mirrors where I pushed Constanza's reflection aside to find my own, to look at my body, to make sure that I had human skin, that my eyes were the same brown colour they had always been, that I was still myself, Constanza, the old one, to make sure that I was human. But the lizard-boy was already inside me, slithering under my skin and into my mind, whispering: '*I knew I was not the only one*.' And even though my face was the same face I always had, my thigh was green, my sex was rotting.

I don't like to be touched. She does. She likes to be touched with the eyes, with the fingers, even with the tongue. Not me. When a man touches me my body turns into salt, bitter and hard, I can almost feel the crystals forming inside me, salt mixed with saliva slowly turning into a briny paste. I fall apart with each thrust and I imagine the crystals scattered all over the bedsheets. I know that one day all the crystals I have lost will leave marks on my body and I'll have a hole in my arm or in my back, a hole that will show where the crystals once were. I might turn into something like the *Victory of Samothrace* – no arms, no head, hopefully wings.

In bed I spend my time feeling ashamed for the salty taste of my skin. I retreat to the back of my mind, away from the hands that burn my arse, from the lips that slime down my back like an oversized mollusc.

I know desire, don't get me wrong, it haunts me like it does everyone else. But her, I know she must grow when she is in bed, no tremors, no cold eyes, no bitter crystals. She dances in bed, I am sure, she folds and unfolds herself over and over. Me? I move carefully not to break apart.

My skin shrinks when it's touched by fingers, fingers that

irradiate a yellow heat – it's always yellow – a heat that extends and paints the salt, leaving behind a trace of its path over me. And there's also the voice inside my head: What's wrong with you? Close your eyes. Kiss back. Open your legs as wide as you can. Don't cover your breasts with your hands. Push back with your hips. Don't look for salt. Don't look for crystals. You are not falling apart. Now whisper. Do something.

I wanted to hurt her. Why wasn't she the one rotting away? Why was she still mocking me from the mirror? You are no longer here, Constanza, do you understand? She did not. I took an ashtray from one of the shelves and threw it against the mirror. It was an ashtray she had given to me almost twenty years ago, a gift she had made at school for Mother's Day. The mirror shattered and the ashtray fell by my feet. My left leg was covered in mildew all the way down to the ankle. I had already lost more than three hours.

Constanza kept looking at me from the shattered mirror now in fragments all over the floor. I told her I planned to go to her house and tell her seven-year-old son that the man he called dad was not his real father. 'Your real father is a son of a bitch who ran away as soon as he found out that your mother was pregnant. And he was not the first one.' I kept talking to her shattered image. 'Then I will call your daughter and once I have them together I will tell them they had an older brother that a doctor sucked out of you with a hose. Have you seen him?' I will ask. 'He often appears around my house. By the way, your mother is a bitch, I am sorry but it is the truth, she is a whore and she is ungrateful. Do you know what that means? It is like a dog that bites its owner, like a son who stabs his father in the back. Yes. That is what she is.'

The reflection laughed. A broken laugh.

The spot grew down my foot like a leech.

Now it's dark outside. We have covered the lamp with a tea towel to dim the light. We want to see but we do not want to see it all.

'You are very quiet all of a sudden,' says Agustina.

I am. I don't know why. It might be that I find confessions a little solemn and a little fake. But talking clears my mind. A bit. It might clear my body too. Who knows. All we can do is wait. When you're caught in a storm you can barely see where you are walking. Pain is like walking under a very heavy rain and struggling to keep the wind from blowing your umbrella away because it is your only shelter, fragile and stupid. And while you fight it is hard to understand that if only you lowered your umbrella you could see the path in front of you, and you would learn that rain does not hurt, it cleanses, it does not attack you, it washes your pain away.

Seventeen hours until Agustina's wedding and my leg was covered in mildew. It no longer tickled, it felt lighter than it ever did before, as if I could run my hand through it, even though I knew it was solid. I pinched one of the white bumps that grew over the mildew. It did not hurt. I ripped it off and held it between my fingers. It felt like a sponge and it was soft. I ate it. I looked down again: three new fat bumps had grown in the place where I had ripped it from.

I am a monster.

I wanted to talk to someone. Anyone. But how could I communicate with normal people now? Should I speak in riddles like a sphinx? Throw darts like a manticore? The truth was that I felt ashamed. Of what? I don't know, but Agustina's wedding was looming and I was no closer to solving this problem.

The ashtray was still on the floor. I picked it up. It was made of modelling clay that had never fully hardened. I squashed it between my hands and turned it into a ball. With the tip of a pencil I drew on it two closed eyes with long eyelashes, a round nose and thick lips. It was the head of a fetus. The outcast child. The life Constanza and I had decided to interrupt. Rafael.

I have a lot of memories of Constanza's abortion: her sweating hand between mine, my breath, the voice of the doctor saying *this might hurt a little, I will clean this now, deep breaths, push, this is the anaesthetic, count to ten*. Goodbye. When death strikes a family one gets disorganised and numb but with Rafael we acted as if nothing had happened. When we left the clinic Constanza and I went to see a movie. I guess we didn't want to look at each other. It might have been easier to acknowledge what had happened – the child is dead – and then cover our faces with ashes and cry. We ran away. Constanza never talked about it again. I should have been surprised by her silence, but I could not tell it apart from my own. She was eighteen years old when she told me she was pregnant. She was not ready to be a mother. The father was an arsehole she met in college who wore his shoes two sizes too big to disguise his small feet and smoked unfiltered Delicados because he thought they made him look tough. He disappeared as soon as he knew she was pregnant. Neither Constanza nor I had any doubt: this child that grows in your belly must go away. But he didn't. Not completely. From time to time I saw the ghost of the fetus and I knew he was looking at me. He liked to hide under Agustina's pillows or in the dogs' blankets. I don't know if anyone else saw him. I doubt it. I am not sure when I started calling him Rafael.

'Where are you, Rafael? Can you hear me? Maybe you are asleep,' I said.

Constanza's reflection finally turned her back on me, in silence.

I put the clay head to my hear, as one does with a seashell. I heard the sound of waves, the amniotic fluid licking the skin of the fetus, waves that reach all around it, the very first touch that its skin feels, waves that adjust to the movement of the world that is its mother. I also heard the rush of blood in the veins across the sky that is her belly: red and black and translucent. And suddenly a new sound: a vacuum that sucks out all the air and the waves, the tide goes down and the water, the blood and the world come to an end.

Holding the clay head in my hand I whispered 'Let's go' and went looking for Rafael.

An empty house is like a sepulchre. A sepulchre with our name. My name. Her name. When I went down the stairs in my own house I felt like I was walking into a place abandoned after being hit by a plague. A ghost town, all the doors open because there is nothing left to protect, no more hands to hold things, no more mouths to eat things, nobody. A place whose inhabitants had died a long time ago, killed by a horrible disease: rotting flesh, dry eyes, exposed teeth. I could almost see my feet walking among the discarded remains of everyday life: an embroidered handkerchief, a bent spoon. Objects that bear witness to our existence and become useless once we are gone.

I wouldn't have been surprised to find a heap of rags covering a pile of human remains. Would my children find me like that?

My house, a ghost town where empty rocking chairs move with the wind, where curtains are useless because once the plague strikes there is no more privacy to guard, all the mirrors are empty and not even the cats survive to wander around in the night.

Was I the plague? Green-skinned woman, black wings

and a dragon tail that sweeps from side to side and strikes whoever crosses its path. I saw mothers trying to protect their children between weak arms, old men collapsed against the walls, vultures circling over their heads.

Was this devastation my own doing? It was me who had the marks all over my body. All I was missing was the empty eye sockets, the long tail.

Who was the monster?

Who was the beast?

Who was the infection?

I even had my first victim.

No, no, no.

Rafael had been something else.

If only he would drop dead, I thought on the night Felipe told me about Constanza, or about what he thought had happened between them. Why can't he just drop dead right now?

We were in the upstairs living room, facing each other with the coffee table as a safety barrier between us. It was two days after I found him having dinner with Constanza. On the coffee table was an open bottle of tequila. I tried to keep his glass full. I was desperate for any kind of advantage over him.

Felipe kept running his hand through his grey hair and drinking shot after shot of tequila. His gnarled hands disgusted me as much as his eyes did. I hated that look of victim he was so good at. Stop. I won't talk about him any more than I have to. Just a little. Just enough. I won't talk about where I met him, I won't say whether I liked him or not. I will not describe his skin, his clothes. I will not say whether I loved him or not. In this recollection he will be little more than a shadow, a stupid shadow, a bad-smelling shadow but a shadow nonetheless.

So we were in the upstairs living room. He knew I was getting ready to attack.

'Constanza told me everything,' I lied.

'What do you mean by *everything*?' he asked.

'Everything,' I repeated.

He was not surprised, his hands did not shake and he didn't spit out the tequila he was drinking. All he did was open his eyes wide, those black eyes that only Agustina inherited.

'All lies,' he said. His voice sounded tired and I almost felt sorry for him. Then I thought: I want to see you squirm.

'What is a lie?' I asked.

'Everything. All lies,' he said.

We were not talking to each other, we just spoke as if we were performing a ritual that had to be gone through. We had to sit in that living room because that's what we did every time there was something to talk about. That's where we sat to choose schools for the children, where we wondered why Leonel wanted to sleep outside with the dogs, where we discussed how to keep Agustina from drawing on the walls. The upstairs living room. So that is where we sat to look into each other's eyes, to feel ashamed and foolish and ask stupid questions, to throw accusations around. We didn't know what else to do.

'Do you love her?'

'Does it matter?'

We were moving in circles. Sometimes he denied everything and the next moment he showed me the songs he had written for her and told me about that afternoon they spent in my studio, about the dresses and the mirror.

He confessed he had dreamt of taking her to a hotel in Reforma and having sex against the window, the city below them. The family below them. He said she sent him silent kisses across the room when I was not looking. He said she smiled to him. He confessed he had asked her to dye her hair red just like mine and she had done it. He said that he knew he was old but she had made him feel alive, wanted.

'Do you know how long it has been since I felt this alive?' he said.

I had to agree that it had been years since his eyes shone like they did when he talked about her. I wanted to put an end to all that light. I wanted to hit him until all the life had left his body. But of course I was only fooling myself. I don't think I had the courage to hit him with my fist.

'Why did she do it?' I asked.

'Because you are not her mother. Because you have other children,' he said.

'And why did you do it?'

'To hurt you. We both did it to hurt you,' he said.

Nothing we said was new but we couldn't stop talking. Felipe kept drinking. I had to stop myself from saying: You've had enough.

'Do you remember when she first came to live with us?' I asked. 'Do you remember how you complained about it? You said: She is not your responsibility, send her back to her mother.'

'I remember.'

'All the fights we had.'

'All the trouble she caused,' he said.

'So what happened? Do you think she has changed? No, Felipe, she is the same troubled teenager only fifteen years older. She is the same girl who used to spend her nights who knows where and who couldn't care less if we were worried about her. She is the same capricious girl you wanted to send back to her mother. Do you remember when she burnt Leonel's hair while he slept?' I said.

'Child's play,' he said.

'So is this.'

'Do you think she did it to fuck me up?' he asked.

'She did it to fuck us all up,' I said. 'No. I don't know. I don't think Constanza spends much time thinking why she does things, you know?'

'I told her I had ruined everything with you. I told her she was my second chance,' he said.

'New woman, same name,' I said.

'That sounds sick.'

'It is.'

We talked like this for hours. The anger. The hate. We talked about it all as if it was not happening to us. What a waste of time. And so much to do. I hope it doesn't rain tomorrow before the tent gets here, the rain might ruin the new grass. He showed me some biology books he had lent her, all filled with graphs, drawings, all marked by Constanza. He imagined secret messages from her in the writing in the margins. We laughed.

'I am acting like a fool,' he said.

'You are.'

The alcohol finally took over his body and after a couple of hours all Felipe could do was close his eyes and cry without tears.

'How did it come to this? How did we let something like this happen?'

The dogs barked. Leonel was in the house. I know I have barely talked about Leonel. I don't want him involved in all this. He is my youngest and I can't help thinking of him as if he were still a boy. Agustina is the same way with him. But he is a grown man, twenty-seven years old, tall and bearded, strong arms. He is a grown man who still drinks a whole litre of chocolate milk every night. He reminds me of my brother Tavo.

We heard Leonel close the front door.

'Mum?' he called.

What was left of Felipe crawled to the bathroom so his son wouldn't see him in such a state. Leonel came upstairs followed by the two grey mastiffs that went everywhere with him.

'Go to the bathroom and help your father. He is not feeling very well,' I said.

He found his father sitting on the bathroom floor.

'He drank too much,' I said.

'How much?' Leonel asked, looking scared. He always looks scared and then he turns into a problem-solving machine until his fear runs out.

'A lot,' I said

'Why didn't you stop him?' he asked, his eyes full of suspicion.

'Because I gave it to him,' I said and held his gaze. I almost heard his brain starting to work, looking for an answer. Felipe was just sitting there at our feet and I felt nothing but contempt for him. How dare you look so defenceless? Fight back!

Very carefully Leonel managed to hold Felipe and drag him to the shower. The water was very cold and it woke him up.

'Dad, you have to throw up,' Leonel said.

'In the shower?' I asked. 'He'll make a mess!'

'Dad, can you hear me? Come on, get on your hands and knees. Help me, Mum.'

'No,' I said.

Leonel managed to make his father lean forward and he wrapped his arms around his waist and pressed his stomach. Nothing. He opened Felipe's mouth and stuck two fingers down his throat. Felipe gagged and puked all over the tiles.

'Good, Dad, get it all out,' Leonel said and stuck his fingers in Felipe's throat again. Felipe's suit was covered in vomit, his tie, his socks. The dogs tried to lick his face but Leonel stopped them. 'It was way too much alcohol, Mum,' he said.

Felipe was shaking under the cold water.

'What if he dies?' I said. 'Do you think this can kill him? Or the cold, he might get pneumonia. Please, God, let him die, let him get pneumonia.'

'Shut up, Mother!'

I continued praying in silence.

Felipe spent a long time under the water while Leonel cleaned his face and the front of his suit.

'Dad, don't fall asleep.'

I stood there as my son brought his father back to life, in spite of my prayers, in spite of the old man's shame. I don't know if it was Leonel's strength or his pity but he managed to help his father get out of the shower by himself and he helped him to a chair. The dogs sat by Felipe's feet as if to warm them. Leonel stripped him and covered his shaking body with a bathrobe.

'Let's take you to your bed,' my son said.

'He doesn't have a bed in this house,' I said.

'I'm fine here,' Felipe mumbled.

'I'm going down to the kitchen to make some coffee. Don't touch him, Mother,' Leonel said.

He came back with a coffee pot and made his father drink cup after cup. He spent the rest of the night by his side, sitting on the floor with the dogs, talking about anything he could think of and saying over and over again: 'Stay awake, Dad, don't fall asleep.'

'Can you hear me, Rafael?'

I looked in all the bedrooms. I searched under Agustina's blankets, in Leonel's shoes. My footsteps on the wooden floors were the only signs of life. 'Rafael!' I kept calling him, but I was not sure that I wanted him to answer. I don't know what I wanted. Company, perhaps. Sixteen hours to go until Agustina's wedding.

Rafael could be anywhere. It's not hard to hide when you are as big as an apple. I found it strange that he wouldn't come out, it always seemed to me that he wanted to be seen: in the silverware drawer, in the waste basket.

I looked behind bookcases and under tables with the feeling of both fear and disgust one has when looking for a cockroach to kill it. I called and called but he did not answer. Good. What would I have done if he had answered? My children might have found me hours later lying on the carpet, white hair, open mouth, hard as a rock. But if I didn't hurry they would find me covered in mildew. Was that any different?

Once I had looked in all the usual hiding places I realised Felipe's guitar case was still there, useless as a corpse lying on the pavement. I told him to get all of his things out of my house, why did he leave precisely that? I always hated that guitar. No, that is not true, that's a lie. There was a time when I liked them both, him and his guitar, over thirty years ago. He was seven years older than me and had a red Mustang that he drove to his office in the centre of the city where you could hear the bells from the cathedral ring every afternoon at six o'clock. I don't want to talk about him. I liked his dark skin, his black beard and his hair, I loved his deep eyes with purple under-eye circles. I liked his strength, his long limbs, his footsteps that almost left footprints on the asphalt. The guitar used to travel on the back seat of the Mustang and once in a while it made a complaining sound so Felipe would reach out and touch it as if to say: It's fine, it was only a bump on the road. It is hard for me to remember him that way, I feel like I am talking about someone else. Perhaps it's everyday life, the dullness that turns everything into wallpaper that no one looks at any more.

Once the songs he wrote were for me. Then they were for someone else. And someone else. Until they reached Constanza, the young one.

The guitar case was there, lying on the sofa, as if it still belonged in my house. While I looked at it the case trembled. I thought I had imagined it but it moved again. I approached it slowly. It moved once more. I touched it with my finger and then pushed it until it fell to the floor. The strings sang, complaining.

'Shut up!'

They sounded again.

'Shut up, you fucking guitar!'

They sounded again.

'This is ridiculous,' I said, and without giving myself any time to think I opened the case and looked at the guitar. I held it by the neck and took it out of the case. Inside the sound hole I saw a glimmer of light.

Rafael.

A cold chill ran down my back. I remembered then that the little one liked to hide inside the guitar, perhaps he liked the darkness or the way the sound reverberated off the wood all around him. I put the guitar back on the sofa and sat beside it.

'Come here.'

The fetus didn't move. Good. I had never touched it and I wasn't even sure that it was solid. Did I want it to come out? Did I want to see him come to me, his head reaching between the strings, his round nose sniffing my breath?

'Come here, little one, come here.'

I reached into the guitar and grabbed him. He squirmed under my touch. I held him in my shaking hand: he was as heavy as an apple and felt warm. This tiny body died twenty years ago, I thought. And I knew that I had crossed a terrible barrier and that it was going to be very hard to return from the other side of who knows where.

'Hello, Rafael.'

I ran my finger down his curved back and saw him move his arms and legs, like a beetle on its back. I felt wetness on my cheeks and only then did I realise I was crying.

Finally I lost control. I knew this because I could not

move. I had no ideas, no plan, I did not say: I'll deal with this. Nothing but fear, pure and white and iridescent, blinding fear. I was not afraid of the tiny body I held in my hand. I was afraid of myself because I could see it and hold it and because I wanted to crush it between my fingers.

He kicked me twice on the thumb and that brought me back from wherever I was headed. The fetus was shaking and I thought he might be cold. I put it on my green leg and when the mildew touched the fetus it grew fast, fertilised, it thickened and seemed to want to warm the fetus. I found the mildew cleaner, less corrupt.

After I sat there for a few minutes I put the fetus on the sofa. With Felipe gone there was no reason for the guitar to be still there. I held it by the neck again and shook it, then I lifted it over my head and slammed it against the floor. I was hoping to see splinters fly all over the living room but only the soundboard cracked. I hit it again and this time the wood did explode and the damned thing complained one last time. As I kept hitting it against the floor the bridge came loose and the strings got tangled. I hit and hit until I held only the headstock.

'No more songs.'

How to get rid of the case? As I held it, a yellow notebook with Felipe's handwriting fell from an inner pocket.

January 24

She is up early. Long wet hair. She went out and sat in the garden under the tree. Was she playing with the dogs or did she want me to see her? I don't know how I managed to stop looking at her and leave for work.

March 14
She is here again. I get dizzy. I act like a fool. She talks about her children and her husband. My children listen to her and my wife asks questions. She talks to them but she smiles just for me.

April 8
I haven't been sleeping. I think Constanza knows something. So does Agustina. She won't talk to me. She won't look me in the eye. How did they find out?

July 25
She left her bedroom door open. I didn't dare go in. The whole family was downstairs. I am a coward.

August 27
She came to town for work. I called and had to wait a long time to get an answer. I just wanted to know how you were doing, I said and hung up. I felt like a fool. An old fool.

November 23
I drove around in circles before I got to her office. Tell her her uncle is here, I told the secretary. She came down to meet me. I brought you some food, I said. How lovely, thank you. She kissed me on the cheek and left. I stood

there in the reception without knowing what to do. I did not like the look the secretary gave me.

Christmas
She was getting ready in her bedroom. She looked out as I walked by and called me in silence. I went. Do I look good? she asked. I sang: You look wonderful tonight. Leonel came upstairs. I hope he didn't hear. I rushed down to the kitchen. I keep her smile.

'Poor old man, she made a fool of you too.'

I held Rafael's neck between my forefinger and thumb, I opened my mouth and put his head between my teeth and felt his trembling back. I bit and felt the neck break like an eggshell. No I didn't. I felt nothing. Laughter came from somewhere between my chest and my stomach. I laughed, half crying, half screaming. I laughed until I could move no more.

'Where is Rafael?'

I went into Agustina's bedroom to lie on her bed, to calm myself down, to cry a little. When Constanza first came to live with us Agustina was not willing to share her bedroom with her. 'I'd rather be by myself,' she said, and moved all her things to the greenhouse at the end of the hall. I thought it was a good idea. We cleared a corner of the greenhouse and put her bed there, under the glass roof. Over the years the plants shared space with the bookcases, her drawing table, her paint cans and brushes. She liked to draw there, with the light coming through the roof and the glass walls. During the winter the room was freezing and during summer the heat was almost unbearable. She didn't seem to mind, always sitting at her drawing table, the plants splattered with ink and paint, the books covered in dirt.

Agustina has a whole bookcase filled with black notebooks she won't let anyone see and I had no idea what was in them. I took one and looked through it. I felt a little guilty and what I found didn't make me feel much better. But I needed to do this. I know my daughter's work, the illustrations she does for children's books. But these notebooks held a whole different range of sketches, all in black and white, pencil and ink, each of them marked with a strange phrase. The first drawing I saw: a wide river with a strong current and three men sitting on sticks in the middle of the river, wearing turbans and tunics. In a corner Agustina floats on a white surface. The caption: *The caterpillar's annihilation has begun.* On a different page I saw a field with dry bushes, dead grass and a burning house in front of which stood a young man, his body burnt, his skin a dry paste falling apart. Agustina is there holding a hose and the writing says: *It's useless but he likes to see me try.* I took down another notebook, hoping to find something, anything, less disturbing. I opened it at a page that showed a dead pig hanging over a counter beside a cartoon Constanza holding a baby pig in her arms. *That's how the March of the Mistaken began.* The last page I looked at had a picture of a street covered in snow and a car in the middle of the road. Inside the car: Agustina and Leonel. Constanza standing in the background. All three of them were looking at a man who was trying to cross the street with two dead children on his back, followed by a woman. *I hope they make it*, read the caption.

Who was this Agustina? I asked myself. I still do. Who is she? Those notebooks were like a nightmare archive. I don't want to talk about Agustina. Who are you? Sometimes I think of her as if she were a part of me, as if we shared something, a foot, a torso. Then I feel that there is something wrong, like waking up one morning to find someone else's arm hanging from my shoulder. Stop. Agustina, the ruffles, look what time it is!

I sat on the floor, among the plants. My green leg smelled like a dark basement, an old closet, it smelled forgotten. I saw then that the mildew had extended beyond my toes and had wide filaments, long like pine needles. From one of my toes a branch was now growing.

Agustina is restless. She goes to pour herself another drink. She is never the same to me; sometimes I see her as a young girl, sometimes as a grown woman. Today she is a woman, small but strong, so like me and so different from me. She is like a bad portrait of my younger self, with mistakes all over the place: darker skin, fuller lips. And she has her father's eyes, those eyes that come from a different time, a different country, where women wear veils over their heads and line their eyes with kohl. Those eyes contain barren lands, bright colours, wars. I would rather not talk about Agustina. Mildew. Concentrate.

My children grew up in a house full of visitors. Agustina used to ask: 'Why does everyone leave and I have to stay here?' Leonel spent all day out in the garden, kicking a ball against the wall, bathing the dogs, sleeping with them in one of their small wooden kennels. Uncles, cousins, family friends, everyone had a room in my house, all running away from divorces, family fights, exile, money trouble. When I wasn't up in my studio working I spent all my time changing bedsheets, stocking the pantry or the fridge, washing towels.

Agustina soon learned not to get attached to the guests and used to say: 'One day I will be the one going away and then you will miss me.'

Agustina, did you ask what time they're delivering the tables and chairs? We have to go over that list again, Agustina, otherwise people won't know where to sit, are you listening to me? She used to have a box under her bed where she hid things she had stolen from the guests: a fountain pen, a single pearl earring, an old photograph. Maybe it was then that she developed her quiet personality, always distant, never fully trusting anyone, forever fearful that happiness could be taken away from her in an instant, forever convinced that all the people she loved would end up walking away from her. 'When will Constanza leave?' she kept asking when she was a child. You really should get some sleep, dear, you have a big day tomorrow.

One night she found me sitting in the garden under the tree, drinking a glass of wine. 'What did he do now?' she asked. 'Constanza,' I answered. She swayed and I feared she might fall but she sat down next to me. We sat there in silence for a long time. It began to rain. We didn't move.

She is back now. She doesn't want to rush me but she is restless, worried, sad. She tries not to look at me while she listens and I try not to think about what her eyes see when she looks at me. It's been a few hours since I last looked in the mirror.

I would rather not talk about you, Agustina.

W*e are all strange creatures. Beauty lies in difference. Who is to say what is normal and what is not?* I have heard and spoken these words over and over again, as if they are a part of becoming a parent. I imagine they are handed down to every woman when their first child is born.

But I am not fooled. I know that we defend difference only when we are not different ourselves. Many of us have counted our children's fingers and toes the minute they were born and we have sighed in relief: our offspring is human. Something deep inside tells us: there are exceptions, not every child is of the same species, there have been hybrids, surprises. But who will admit to giving birth to a monster?

A long time ago mothers would pray to their family gods for a human child. Many hybrids were broken against the sharp teeth of a mountain cliff; others inhaled their first breath only to exhale their last, smothered under the blankets. What, then, would one do with a boy covered in scales? What to do with a girl that had the witch's sixth finger? With a little luck we would say: diseases, anomalies, infections.

I sat among the plants in Agustina's bedroom, thirteen hours before her wedding, and I looked at my green leg and at my foot with its tiny branch and I thought: this is not entirely disgusting, it might even be beautiful, like a tree trunk by a lake, a thick root from an old tree. Many white bumps had grown over the green vegetation. And even if this was part of a body, my body, worse things had happened to human skin before, all kinds of creatures had walked the earth. Maybe this mildew was not a terrible thing; if there were people allergic to light then I could manage with a rotting leg. But could I?

I thought about those pictures of skin diseases and wondered if they were really illnesses. They might be something else entirely. The lizard-boy could really be a lizard. That other picture of a foot with a layer of white crystals growing on it could be a miniature cliff where miniature albatrosses nested. Why not? Each one of those bodies was a different creature and each bleeding scar that looked like a leech, each spot shaped like a cloud or a mushroom, they could all be a voyage, a mutation, an evolution.

Constellations of red birthmarks, a girl with her back covered in black spots like a leopard, a woman with a melted face, a man with bubbles of skin all over his body, someone with sand under their armpits – they could all mean something, they could be a step forward or backward, they could be what survived of creatures that had become extinct. Could the lizard-boy be a descendant of a *quetzalcoatl?*

The mildew might not be a curse. It could be an exit.

I fell asleep in Agustina's bedroom and when I woke up both my legs were covered in green, two beautiful trunks coated in mildew with green needles growing on my toes. The light bouncing on my vegetation and playing with the small white bumps made my legs iridescent, kaleidoscopic. Two wonderful green legs, organic, majestic. They seemed to want to move by themselves, without a torso, perhaps without me. I could almost see them dancing around on stage, making turns and jumps and falling down on the floorboards. I felt proud, as if I had made them.

I couldn't stop touching them, perhaps because if I didn't I could not feel them, my body was numb from the waist down. There was no more tickle, no pain, only absence. If I didn't look at my legs, if I didn't touch them, they did not exist. But at the same time I knew they were indomitable, they could jump on rocks and swim in a wild, cold river where the filaments would close and filter the air, the water, the pain. My pain. They were ancient specimens dating back to the first forms of life that were not yet animals, not yet plants, still full of possibilities.

I was half monster, half woman, a demon perhaps, or a deity, an imagined creature.

And I liked it.

I noticed I could not move my left foot when I tried to go down the stairs. I wanted to eat something but before going down I stopped to look at the pictures that hung on the staircase. Why do we hang them there? Perhaps because it's a space without definition, it's not a bathroom or a kitchen, perhaps because no one wants the faces of uncles and grandparents looking at their faces or their backs while they sleep.

From the top of the stairs I could see the picture of my grandmother Loreto, framed in gold, at the bottom of the stairs. I wanted to go down and look at it but I tripped. My left foot, which only a minute ago was light and strong, was now a dead weight. I grabbed onto the banister and tried to stand up but I lost my balance again. Hanging from the banister I pulled my right leg towards me and felt it heavy, like green marble. I tried to move my toes, which were no longer tiny branches but had turned into a mass of white needles with black tips, a gigantic dandelion. Where were my toes? I couldn't move them because I didn't know exactly where they were under that white vegetation that looked as if it belonged under the sea. How could it be so heavy when it looked so frail? I touched it, it was colder than my hands, colder than my breasts. I ripped a filament and a thick white pus oozed from its base.

My grandma Loreto looked at me from her picture.

'Shit, grandma, what happened to us?'

My grandma Loreto was a tiny woman who had two obsessions: her head and her left hand. Her obsession with her head was understandable – from the time she was a girl she suffered from severe migraine attacks that kept her from moving and turned her into a big complaining heap. I remember her with her hand clasped at the side of her face, her eyes black and empty like those of a fish in a frying pan. *Keep quiet, mama Loreto has a headache. Don't shout, don't play the piano, tonight we'll have to use candles at the dinner table because mama Loreto can't bear the light.*

Her obsession with her left hand was not that clear. My grandma spent her last years worried about something that she found terrifying: she had a very short life-line on the palm of her hand. She told any one who would listen: 'Look, can you see this line here, close to the thumb? That one is the life-line and it shows how long one gets to be around here, but mine stops right in the middle of my hand, can you see it? It starts here and then it stops, just like that, see? That means I will die young.'

I used to look at her wrinkled face, at her hands covered in age marks. Die young? Once I told her: 'Grandma, you will not die young because you are no longer young!' And that same hand with its short life-line struck me in the face.

Those nights on which Loreto didn't have a migraine she sat in the living room next to the lamp and drew in her notebook the palm of her hand, measuring each line with a wooden ruler she had stolen from my school bag. She spent hours deep in her calculations, like an alchemist. She placed all her instruments on the table and cleaned each pencil with her skirt. My brothers and sisters made fun of her but to me that ritual was a mystery – only when she lost herself in her calculations did her hair came loose from her tight bun, only then did she remove her high-heeled shoes and loosen her dress, only on those nights under the light of her lamp did my grandma lose her absent manner and her eyes came alive with a look of determination that fascinated me.

Hidden behind her chair, I heard her say: 'The lines change, they grow, they always have a different message, they have to change, why can't this line grow longer?' But neither her palm nor mine changed at all and the stubborn life-line on my grandma's hand remained short.

The funny thing was that Loreto knew nothing of chiromancy. The obsession had struck her out of nowhere and my mother fired the cook because she thought it had been her idea. She even forbade Loreto to listen to the radio: God only knows what crazy ideas they broadcast. My father, on the other hand, gave Loreto a book on divination that he had ordered from his book dealer in Mexico City. My grandma looked at it, confused. 'What do you want me to do with this?' she asked. 'It's for your calculations, Doña Loreto, so you can learn more about it all.' My grandma turned her back on him. 'I know all I need to know, thank you,' she said and walked away. But she didn't know a thing, she had invented her own method: ablutions with goat's milk, midnight rubs with red wine vinegar, black lace gloves on nights when there was a full moon.

Once, my sister Flor took grandma Loreto's notebook and erased the life-line from the last pages. That night a cold shriek ran through the house and when we all went to look for grandma Loreto we found her gripping her notebook and suffering one of her worst migraines. She could hardly see, and the mere sound of our slippers on the floor made her vomit. 'My time has come, the line, the line is gone!' she said. A trickle of urine ran down her legs and I also wet myself.

Grandma Loreto died while I was in boarding school and no one thought to let me know. But her obsession had been passed on to me. I soon discovered a small graveyard behind the chapel and spent my lessons wondering if the nuns buried there had had long or short life-lines. Once, armed with a spoon that I had stolen from the dining room, I managed to sneak out to a recent grave and I had dug a hole almost a foot deep in the ground when a nun found me and dragged me by my braids to the Mother Superior's office. Sick, perverse, diabolical, they called me. 'Mother Inés, God have mercy on her soul, will come in the middle of the night to disturb your sleep, to cover your head with a pillow, to pull at your feet for having dared to disturb her holy sepulchre,' they said. But she never came.

One week before the mildew there was a message on the answering machine: 'Hello, aunt, it's Constanza. Please stop calling me. I won't answer.'

Agustina was the first to hear the message. 'Mum, that degenerate bitch called you,' she said.

I played the message several times. Aunt? She always called me Constanza, just Constanza. I called her, of course. I dialled once, twice, three times, until I had memorised the number. You will answer, you'll see. She didn't. I went out to look for a pay phone so she couldn't recognise the number I was calling from. I dialled. This time she answered.

'It's Constanza,' I said.

'Same here.'

'You will come to my house and we will settle this once and for all,' I said.

'I'm sorry, aunt, I have to work.'

'I'll wait.'

'No, aunt, I'll be working most of the night,' she said.

'It doesn't matter. I'll wait.'

'And I'm meeting a friend for drinks,' she said.

'When you are done, you'll come here.'

'I won't.'

'You will. I'll be waiting. And I won't call again. Let me know when you are on your way, no matter what time it is, understood?'

'Yes.'

I spent the afternoon working on Agustina's wedding dress. I traced the skirt, I cut the corset and marked the darts under the chest. I tried not to think of Constanza so I wouldn't sew all my hatred and disgust into the dress. When the phone rang it was past two in the morning. 'It's me, do you still want me to come?' 'Yes,' I said.

A few minutes later I went downstairs to open the door. I didn't want her to use her own key. She looked beautiful. When she came close to kiss me I could smell alcohol. She had drank as much as I had, to give herself courage.

'Come upstairs to the studio,' I said.

'The studio?' She almost laughed.

She followed me anyway.

'I'm exhausted, can we do this fast?' she asked.

'Do what?' I locked the door behind us.

'All this drama.'

'Do you think this is all a drama?'

'Stop it, Aunt, get to the point, this is getting boring.'

'Why don't you begin, if you are in such a rush?' I said.

'Fine. Your husband tried to take advantage of me. Here.' With a gesture she pointed to the studio, the fabric, the dress forms, the fake eyes of the mannequins.

Now I laugh at your solemn face, your hands bunched into fists, your white knuckles. Who were you? Constanza the orphan, Constanza the teenager who whispers in Agustina's ear, 'I should be your mother's daughter, my skin is white like hers, unlike yours.' Constanza the young woman who was always late to collect Leonel from school: 'Don't cry like a girl, are you a faggot?' You were funny, Constanza, sitting there with that threatening manner. But I was even funnier because I was breaking.

'He made a move on me that time I came to collect the dresses and he offered me a beer. I knew what he was after and I thought: I'll fuck you up, old man, I'll make a fool of you. And he said: Do you want to be my young Constanza?'

You contradicted yourself, you got lost. And so did I. I almost took your word for the truth because I wanted to believe you. But you were so stupid, Constanza, that you couldn't hide the smile that leaked through your teeth.

'Why did you come back here, then?' I asked.

'Where?'

'Here. Why did you come back to the house? All these years. Why do you have dinner with him? Why do you drink wine with him?'

'I do it for you. For Leonel. For Agustina. I didn't want to tear the family apart. I could. I can. But I won't. I don't want to hurt you.' Her words were tangled and desperate.

That's what you said, Constanza, and then you pretended to cry. Please!

'He was obsessed with me. It happens to me sometimes. I have that effect on men. But this is too much. This is family. This is sick,' she said.

‘You were over thirty. You are not a little girl.’

‘He took advantage of me anyway, he knew I thought of him like a father.’

You seemed to have all the answers, Constanza, or so you believed. Youth wouldn’t let you see that inside an older woman the soul is the same as it always was. I am the same woman I was when I was twenty, thirty, your age. I had control of my body in the way one can only have after turning thirty, when one knows what to do with those impulses, with the mouth, with the smell. Now that my age has left traces on my face you wanted to measure yourself up against me. But the soul and the mind are still the same, Constanza, and you had no way of knowing that. Not yet. Inside me live all the women I have been and we are many, many more that you ever were, we are an army.

You were a sad spectacle but I was even worse because I feared you. We were the only spectators of this embarrassing play, you and me and the white mannequins, disembodied heads and arms, the wardrobe of countless plays. And the mirrors pregnant with your image.

Constanza was never a baby. Not to me. I didn't carry her inside my body, I never had the power over her that all mothers have: the power of death. Perhaps that is why I never knew you were so weak, Constanza, because for me you were never small enough to hold a pillow over your head until you stopped breathing.

When she came to me she was already a fully formed being, a small beast that ran and cut her own hands with a razor blade. I had no choice with you, Constanza, you were too old for me to toy with the idea of leaving you in a supermarket or on a park bench.

I had to learn your signs, your code. We didn't make them up together. I didn't impose them on you. You were like the offspring of a giraffe that jumps from the womb to the ground and gets on its feet straight away. You arrived ineluctable, a talking doll, a moving doll that locks baby Leonel inside the refrigerator.

What have we done to you, Constanza? Where are you? Agustina, come here, don't walk away, I can't talk too loud any more. Shorter. Shorter.

A couple of months after Rafael's expulsion Constanza began searching desperately for something, but she didn't know exactly what she needed. I don't blame her. The pain stuck to our skin like fine powder.

She grew interested in acting. I have spent over twenty years in the theatre and I have seen many young girls come close, become trapped and enchanted by the theatre, by those vaults that magnify the voice, by the darkness in which one feels either a caress or a stab, by the ritual, all those eyes on your creation and the audience out there, intimate and distant. Theatre is a well one falls into by accident and then cannot leave. What else can I say after I have spent twenty years sewing the skin of so many characters?

One day Constanza announced she had joined the university's theatre group. She was a student of biology. She was thrilled by the intimate exercises, by spending the afternoon touching a classmate's face, his neck, and letting him touch her. She loved memorising her lines, or the times when she had to walk around the room pretending to be a duck or a pregnant woman. She came home full of energy, happy to have found a place where it was fine to be someone else, to learn new gestures, new expressions, new ways to move and walk. Then came the betrayal. Constanza, you were a magnet for upsets.

They were working on a very ambitious play for a group of amateurs: *Jacques, or The Submission,* by Ionesco. Constanza managed to get a big role: Roberta III, a woman with three noses who Jacques falls in love with and to whom he gives his hat as a sign of commitment – at least that was how Constanza interpreted the play, she never wanted to ask me for advice. 'Stay out of it,' she said when I offered to help her. 'We know what we are doing and we have a teacher, you are not the only one who knows about theatre.'

It was after the rehearsal of an erotic scene that Constanza broke from the theatre for ever. It was a pity – all that anger, all that confusion, all that hunger for love, could have turned her into a wonderful actor. I have seen it happen many times before. Pain never fails when it comes to theatre. It was almost nine o'clock at night and they had spent several weeks rehearsing the same scene: Constanza was riding Jacques' back, she wore a white nightgown she had stolen from Agustina's closet, he had only a pair of pajama trousers on and his chest was naked. They were tired and didn't understand why they had to do that scene over and over again. 'We must be terrible at it,' Constanza said every night. The director of the play was a Dramatic Literature teacher who sat in the back rows of the theatre, in the dark, and kept saying, 'Let's take it from the top.'

Constanza had asked Agustina to pick her up that night and my daughter waited outside for a long time but when no one came out she decided to take a look inside. She walked in and found that only the stage was lit. She saw Constanza all sweaty on Jaques' shoulders and heard her tell the story of a small white bunny. Later she told me that Constanza was an amazing actor: alive, radiant, strong and happy. As Agustina walked closer to the stage to get a better look she discovered the director sitting there in the dark and she heard her moan with her hands under her skirt, between her legs. Without a word Agustina went outside to wait for Constanza.

'I don't believe you, you are jealous of me!' shouted Constanza when they got home and Agustina told us what she had seen. She threw books at us, pillows, shoes. 'You are lying, why would you want to take this away from me?'

Something broke that night between them. Constanza cried all night like she should have cried when we got rid of Rafael. She seemed to be closing some strange parenthesis; it was once again that night when we came back from the clinic, that night we should have spent awake, that time when I didn't run my hand through her hair and I failed to tell her that everything was going to be fine.

She never went back to the theatre, not even to see the plays for which I had designed the costumes. We had betrayed her. The theatre, Agustina and me.

She hardly ever spoke about theatre again and when I threatened to denounce the director she said, 'Don't you dare!' I didn't. It was up to her. I don't know what she told the other students in the group when she quit. But the search didn't stop there, she wanted to replace all that she had lost when she quit the theatre group, the bodies of strangers, the intimacy of sharing stories and pains. She lost herself in idiotic rituals in which she seemed to find solace. She danced in the town squares with groups of young men with naked torsos and seashells tied to their legs; she meditated in the Espacio Escultórico, she drew a blue triangular eye on the ceiling above her bed.

She was lost.

It's pain, I told myself every time I saw her walking out with her hair tangled and the traces of who knows what substance in her eyes, away from us, away from the house that one morning had seen her leave with a child in her belly and at night saw her return hollow.

It was fear, Constanza, it was emptiness.

I told her I could help her get in touch with serious people who were involved in esoteric activities. I was a young woman in the Seventies and worked among artists, I knew the difference between charlatans and serious people. Constanza wouldn't listen to me. 'I have had enough of your suggestions, thank you,' she said.

She didn't want commitments, she wanted to try everything and she did. She spent hours cooking herself up inside a *temazcal*, naked and accompanied only by men, to get in touch with her masculine side. She sat in the centre of a circle surrounded by people she barely knew and after eating some herb she dived down inside her own memory where she found that she had the soul of a bat and she had to stand on her hands and shriek something that sounded like *mama*.

One time she came home with a black eye and her arms covered in scratches. 'Confrontation therapy,' she said. 'One of the girls in my therapy group had to pretend she was my mother and when she said *goodbye* I hit her as hard as I could. It turns out she too had some unresolved issues – see how she left me. Don't look at me like that, this is all led by a professional and once the session was finished we all went for a drink in peace.'

I tried not to laugh at her, at her hands painted with henna, at the air of superiority with which she looked at us all. Children are like that, a little idiotic, a little sweet. I thought she would grow out of it.

It was hard to keep up with her. One day she was fully committed to a group of women who gathered in the woods in Viveros to hug the biggest tree and the next she called them *middle-class idiots*. She hung a crystal in every window of the house to avoid God knows what bad energy and a couple of months later she forgot all about them and told me it was silly to believe in crystals when what the house really needed was Feng Shui.

To stop her pestering us, we went along with her ideas at first, everyone but Agustina. We sprinkled our sheets with clove and lavender essences to lure *nauhuals* closer, and we dressed in yellow on the last night of the month to make our eagle-knights protect us. We did it all to please her. I found her search legitimate; she might have inherited it from my grandma Loreto with her goat's-milk ablutions. But I soon discovered that what Constanza really wanted was to make herself feel superior.

Constanza and Agustina kept growing apart, if they had ever been close. One night after a fight in which they almost hit each other, Agustina found a bowl under her bed that contained sand and a deformed ginger root that looked suspiciously like a mandrake. 'Your boarder has lost her marbles,' she told me, and threw the charm out the window.

You were so naive, Constanza.

Her obsessions kept multiplying. A little before she left the house to go on a long trip around the world she wanted a yellow crescent tattooed between her breasts. I talked her out of it and two weeks later she said that it was unthinkable to harm one's body, a temple, with needles and ink.

She travelled for almost a year. Everyone in the house felt relieved when she left, even if Felipe kept complaining that Constanza was spending a lot of money.

She sent postcards regularly.

Hawaii, 1988
I am far, very far away from home and I feel great. I thought I would feel sad and I am sure you did too. But look at me. I am calm and happy. This place is out of this world and I will start some classes in the local university. Today I move into the dorms, I met a guy who said I could move in with him which is great and a lot cheaper than an apartment for myself. I am fine, people here are beautiful and I think they somehow get me. I hate english, I am terrible at it.

Constanza

Vienna, 1988
I wanted to say hi. It's summer but I am cold. It's June 16 and you forgot my birthday for the first time. Agustina forgot as well. Leonel sent me a picture of the dogs. I still haven't found a Jacques who wants to give me his hat.

Constanza

Montreal, 1988

I am closer now but I feel very far away. Don't forget me. Montreal is very European. The festival goes on day and night and I walk in the streets alone. It is nothing like the US. People are nice and they all look different. I plan to visit an art museum, I'll get you a present. The hostel I found is great, I have my own tiny room with zinc and a shower. I could live here or in Europe. I haven't decided but I'll let you know when I do. I can speak a little french now! Say hi to everyone for me.

Constanza

A fly hits its head against a window, it flies back, gathers speed and hits again. Fly, hit, fly, hit. Behind it is an open room with two doors that lead to other rooms, all possible exits, all with windows that might be open. But the fly insists it will go through the glass, it can see the garden from here, so close, and it will cross that invisible barrier that stops it. Fly, hit, fly, hit. It is condemned to die here, to fall onto the window ledge exhausted, its wings trembling one last time, and still it keeps going, it will not turn around, it will not fly away. Its head hurts, or perhaps it doesn't, who could know? My head hurts and I hit it against this mildew, I lick it, I touch it. Fly, hit.

No, I'm telling you it is not me, it's this fly. My head doesn't hurt. It does. A little, give me something, anything. And go to bed, dear, you have a horrible day ahead of you. I mean a long day, dear, a long day, please don't nag me, Agustina. A long and beautiful day tomorrow. We must finish attaching the ruffles. You must finish. Mildew. Concentrate. And the lights, don't forget the lights that go under the tent. I can do it by myself, I told you I could organise the wedding by myself. Well, dear, I wasn't counting on this, was I? Listen to me. The lights go first, before the tent, because they have to hang them from the tree. Yes, yes, mildew, I am concentrating, but please open the window so that fly can escape.

I reached the ground floor. My left leg was useless. Twelve hours to Agustina's wedding. I looked at those wooden steps that we had walked up and down for decades. On the fourth step Leonel had split his head open, a scar still visible on his temple. I almost fainted when I saw him covered in blood. A bit higher I could see the stain of some paint Agustina had dropped. But those steps were part of a different life, my legs could no longer climb them; they were made for feet, not for white sea urchins. The top floor was unreachable for me now. Perhaps with a rope or by crawling up the walls I could reach the bedrooms, even my studio. But why? My universe was now split in two: up and down. I had nothing to do upstairs, I had all I needed down here. I had nothing.

A door slammed upstairs. I like those inexplicable noises that haunt old houses, the doors closing by themselves, the sound of footsteps on the wooden floors. It's the air, it's the wood, we learn to say.

The garage door opened. Someone was driving in. My leg was very heavy, white needles growing. I dragged myself to the door and locked it just as Agustina was turning the door handle. She looked at me through the glass.

'What is it? Why are you naked?' she asked.

'Don't come in.'

I couldn't lock her out of the house. I had to show myself. I had been lucky enough that one day before the wedding no one had stopped by the house. And it might not be a bad idea to have some company. Besides Rafael and the lizard-boy.

'Go to the back door,' I said.

I didn't know if I should cover myself or remain as I was. I had to move but my leg was a bush of needles and was growing heavier and heavier. I dragged my leg to the kitchen and waited there, watching the glass door that led to the garden. Agustina was about to walk around the house and look at me. It was real now. I hit my foot, or what was once my foot, against the table and the white pus oozed again. For a second I could see two of my toes, two of my toenails, and then, in an instant, they were covered by that stubborn vegetation. Well, at least I was whole under all that white and green.

Agustina approached slowly and stopped at the door. She didn't open it, she didn't move. Her eyes seemed to grow. It was all she did. She drank me in with those black eyes, as if I were a painting and she wanted to commit every brushstroke to memory.

'Shit,' she mumbled.

We stood there for a long time, I can't say how long. She didn't come in, I didn't go out. Neither of us tried to open the door.

'What is it?' she asked and sat on the step that led to

the garden. I sat, or I fell, next to her, with the glass door between us.

'Mildew,' I said.

'Did you make it?'

'I don't think I did.'

'Is it fake? Is it for a play?' she asked.

'No.'

'Did it grow on your skin?'

'Yes.'

'When?'

'Today. Now. It's still growing.'

'Does it hurt?'

'No. Not at all.'

The sun, turning orange, began its descent, dying, while my daughter examined my body inch by inch. The afternoon seemed to want to rob the plants of their colours and they shook slowly.

'Is this because of what we did?' Agustina asked.

I am here and I go and I come back. Agustina paces back and forth, or is it Constanza? My eyes hurt and my head hurts and then nothing hurts.

I am in Chapultepec: the trees, the balloons, the cotton candy, the children running around. My children play in the bushes. By my side there is a young couple, I think I am with them because they speak to me, they also have a boy and a girl. The mother's blond hair frames her pale face, her blue eyes. I come close to her and when she looks at me I know she is threatening me in silence.

Leonel plays baseball with this woman's daughter, he swings the bat and it hits the girl in her right eye. I see the impact: the flesh wrinkles, the bone breaks like an eggshell. The girl falls to the ground and has a seizure. All the children surround her and watch in awe while their equal dies. Some smile. No one cries. The girl shakes on the ground and she is all blond curls and red ruffles.

She is still now.

I fear the mother.

Leonel is sailing in a boat on the lake and next to me is a man, my husband but not Felipe. Leonel goes round and round in the boat and when he comes close I want to warn him about some danger related to his teeth and the lack of food and falling asleep at the wheel, all together like that in a strange logic that I seem to understand. I shout but he can't hear me, he is close to the centre of the lake and far away from me.

The brother of the dead girl is nearby, I can't see him now but he wants to kill my boy. I don't know how I know it but I do. I look for Leonel and I can't find him, he is no longer in the boat. There is a cliff by the lake. The brother of the dead girl looks down. I run, I take him by the arm. 'What happened?' I shake him. He tells me that Leonel's dog ran straight to the edge of the cliff and fell and my son went after him. I look down and there they are, broken on the ground.

'Mother,' Agustina says, 'you are not making any sense.'

The night of the accident I didn't ask many questions. Why would I? We had to move fast. Get her out of the way. I didn't ask because I didn't want to. It was clear to me. Yes, Agustina, it was clear to everyone.

I got home late after a show, it was the opening night and I felt happy and tired. All the lights were off. I heard music coming from the kitchen. I called but no one answered. Someone must have forgotten to turn off the radio, I thought. I went to the phone and played the messages: the first one was from my mother, who was convinced that her nurse was stealing the silver teaspoons again; the second message was from Felipe, who said he would come by after eleven to get the rest of his things.

I was hungry. The dining room was dimly lit by the floodlights in the garden. On the table I found a heap of old photographs. In many of the photographs I could see Constanza and myself. The music kept playing from the kitchen, a piano and a violin that repeated a couple of notes over and over again like a lullaby. In one of the photos I saw myself and Constanza, almost nine years before, walking away in the Chihuahua desert, our feet lost in the hot sand. A much older photograph showed Felipe's old Mustang decorated with balloons, ribbons and paper butterflies, and sitting on the roof was Constanza, a little girl, wearing a purple dress and smiling, holding Felipe's hand, Felipe who still had black hair and a thick moustache, his other hand holding a camera. It was the spring carnival. A whole side of the table was covered in photographs of a very young Constanza with that smile that held no grudges, no absences.

The music, that timid yet persistent music, seemed to call me: come. Yes, yes, there was music, Agustina, I tell you I heard it. I wanted to continue looking at the photographs but I walked to the kitchen, following the music. At first I saw nothing out of the ordinary: the lights of the garden, the grass, the kitchen table. But the kitchen door was open. I went closer and then I found them: Constanza on the ground, her body on the grass, her head on the step, and Agustina seated beside her, her arms around her legs, her hair on her face, humming that tune that was becoming unbearable.

What game are they playing? I thought like a fool, but part of me knew that the stain around Constanza's head wasn't her hair and nor was it the door mat. 'Agustina?' I whispered.

She was strange there, like a dwarf, like a gnome. She raised her head and looked at me without looking. She had three long scratches on her cheek. When she finally recognised me she smiled.

I want to forget that smile.

I felt cold. My two daughters on the ground and all I

could think was: I want a sweater. The music, the dining-room table with the photographs and behind me the dark house. I want a sweater.

'We can't stay here like this,' I said. 'Leonel will be here soon. And Felipe is coming to get his things.'

Agustina – was it Agustina? – wasn't listening to me. I wanted to act fast, before fear took over my mind. I'll deal with it. I wanted to shake Agustina to make her react but to get to her I had to step over Constanza and that was too much. I stood where I was. I'm cold, I want a sweater.

'What happened?'

My daughter smiled again that horrible smile, her hair tangled, her hands like claws on her knees.

'We argued,' she said at last. 'She was strange, she must have been on something, as usual. Do you think she is all right?'

It was clear to me that Constanza was far from all right.

'We argued. I pushed her away and she fell. It was an accident. She was on something, I know she was.'

My God, what is happening here. Rafael was crouched on his mother's chest. Agustina, my Agustina, was humming on the floor.

'Wake up, please wake up,' I prayed.

'We are awake, mother, all three of us,' Agustina said.

'Not all three of us,' I said.

'Move over to that side, I'm coming in,' Agustina said.

We got up. She opened the door and walked past me without touching me, without looking at my legs, at my branches, and went to the refrigerator. All she could find was a chunk of cheese and half a bottle of white wine.

'Don't you eat any more?' she asked.

'I didn't have time.'

'Mum, what happened to you?'

I thought she'd never ask, I thought she would continue to play tough. Or blind.

'I don't know,' I said.

'But you have to know. Is it a disease? Did you call a doctor?' She was crying now, angry. 'How is it possible that you don't know what this is when it's growing all over you?'

I moved closer to hug her, fearing she would reject me. It was very hard to move now, my other foot was heavy and from the knees down it was hard to distinguish my human form. Agustina saw me move towards her. She was so pale I thought she was about to faint.

'Are you sure it doesn't hurt?' she asked when I reached her.

'I am. It's just getting heavier, I think soon I won't be able to move.'

'This is nonsense, Mum. What about tomorrow? What about the wedding? Why did you have to do this right before the wedding?'

'Calm down, dear, we still have some time.'

'Time for what? Time to make you a skirt and move you around on a cart?'

'Time for something.'

Can you hear that? Someone is shouting. Can you hear that? I think it's Leonel. 'Mum, the dogs!' I am in the garden and on the grass lie dogs cut in half. I walk among them, I think there are more than twenty. I stand next to the upper half of a mastiff, its eyes are open and it's shaking. It looks at me with its green eyes and I shiver when I look at the clean cut below its ribs. It doesn't bleed. It's close to death but it moves its remaining legs to touch my foot. Its pain is mine. In silence it is asking me to help it although we both know there is nothing left to do. It dies, it dies! I walk on. The halved dogs shake in agony and I try to keep them company in their last moments but there are so many! What happened here? Leonel is sitting on the ground, his legs crossed, his head in his hands. 'Constanza, Mum, it was Constanza. She wanted to mow the lawn and she killed the dogs. She killed them all.'

'Mother, can you hear me?' Agustina wets my face with cold water. Of course I can hear you. Shorter, shorter. Come, walk with me down this street, this is where I lived as a child in Chihuahua. Look, a woman's head, barely connected by a nerve to a shoulder and an arm. The rest of her body is scattered all over the street. Look how dirty you are. This is a leg, those are fingers, this is what? An ankle, perhaps. I think her face is my face. Can you hear what she says? No, no, don't wet my face, Agustina, I am fine, nothing hurts, of course I'm not having a stroke, what nonsense is that. My father had the stroke, I am fine, I can sing a whole song from beginning to end. Don't wet my face, dear, I'm fine, I'll take care of it.

'Get up Agustina,' I said, trying to keep a steady voice. 'You must get up.'

'Make her move first,' she said, and with the tip of her foot she pushed Constanza's leg. 'You heard, move!' She was acting all weird, sleepy, dragging out the words, and I don't think she could understand what I was saying. 'Don't pay attention, Mum, it must be one of her dramas.'

Agustina got up and pulled Constanza by the legs. 'Get up, dammit! You are worrying my mother!' She pulled Constanza's leg and took off one of her shoes. 'I think she passed out.' Agustina kneeled and leaned very close to Constanza's face to see if she was breathing. Both women had scratches on their faces and arms; a thin red line ran down my daughter's neck from her head to her chest. Constanza's blouse was torn and she had a chunk of Agustina's hair clutched in her hand.

'What has she done now?' asked Leonel, standing behind me.

'Who's there?' shouted Felipe from the front door. 'Why are all the lights off?' He walked into the kitchen.

Someone moaned. We all stood still.

'Please tell me she fell,' said Leonel, holding his father's arm. I don't know if he was about to fall or if he feared his father would run away.

No one spoke for a while – seconds, hours, who knows. Felipe was the first to move, he offered his hand to Agustina and she jumped backwards. 'Don't touch me,' she said. Felipe leaned over Constanza.

'Don't touch her,' I spat.

'We can't leave her on the ground,' he said.

The dogs came into the kitchen and walked around Constanza. One of them licked the dark puddle around her head. 'Out!' shouted Leonel, and the dogs went to the garden.

Felipe touched Constanza's wrist to see if she had a pulse and when he found none he looked at Agustina for a long time before he asked: 'How long has it been? She's no longer warm.'

Agustina groaned and said, 'No.'

'We need to get her out of the way,' Felipe said in a low voice.

I wasn't sure if he meant Constanza or Agustina. Felipe put Constanza's shoe back on and held her by the ankles, careful to do it over her clothes so he wouldn't have to touch her skin.

'Where do we take her?' I finally asked.

'Under the tree.'

Without stopping to think and with my eyes on Agustina, who was almost grunting to the sound of that music still coming from who knows where, I held Constanza by the arms, trying not to touch the puddle that framed her head.

'Are you sure,' I asked.

'Of course I'm not,' said Felipe.

She was heavier than I expected and it took a while to take her to the tree. The garden seemed endless. Constanza's hair swept the grass and I stepped on it by accident. Her head fell backwards and I thought she was looking at me. Rafael was still on his mother's chest and I tried to keep him from falling.

'Leonel, get the shovel,' said Felipe when we reached the tree. We lowered Constanza onto the grass.

'Why me?' asked Leonel, who was very close to his sister but looked afraid to touch her.

'Get it,' I said. I didn't recognise my children. Who were they?

Dragging his feet, Leonel got the shovel from behind the dogs' kennels. The two mastiffs walked around us in circles, their eyes on Constanza. They knew. Felipe took the shovel and began to dig.

'Isn't that the place where we buried Tomas?' Leonel asked. He was standing by his sister once again.

'I think there's at least a metre and a half of dirt before we reach solid rock,' Felipe said. He continued to dig.

Slowly the hole grew deeper. Agustina came close and stood beside me. Leonel took the shovel and dug for a while; his white shirt was soon covered in mud and grass stains. When the hole was a metre deep Leonel found in the dirt a heap of dog bones and a collar.

'I told you this place was taken,' Leonel murmured and very carefully wrapped the bones in his jacket. Then he went back to work and when he got tired I jumped in. The hole was deep and within a few minutes both my legs were covered in dirt.

'That's enough,' Felipe said a while later.

'No, keep going,' Agustina said.

Felipe took the shovel again and dug a little longer, then Leonel helped him out of the hole.

'How do we lower her into the hole?' asked Felipe.

'Just give her a push,' Agustina said. Leonel wrapped his arm around his sister's shoulders and covered her mouth with his hand.

Felipe and I carried Constanza to the edge of the hole. He got inside and very carefully, almost lovingly, as if she were a baby and we were giving her a bath, we lowered her into the earth. I wanted to go upstairs and look for a beautiful dress to bury her in. I didn't. Felipe combed her hair over her shoulders, said something in a very low voice and kissed her on the forehead.

Agustina broke free from her brother's embrace and came closer. Leonel was the only one who cried when Felipe began to cover the hole. I saw Rafael wrapped around his mother's neck, eyes closed, moving his legs and arms, nestling his head against Constanza's ear. Goodbye, Rafael.

The white needles have reached my hand. Agustina helps me drink a little water. Is it Agustina? She has Leonel's hands. But I haven't seen Leonel all day long, all week long, where has he gone? Will the tents be on time tomorrow? It might rain. I hope it doesn't rain. What if it rains? The new layer of grass we put down last week will come loose. What if it rains? I can hear raindrops. The garden will turn to mud.

Sitting at the kitchen table we looked at the glasses of whisky that Leonel gave us. He was the only one drinking, and he was on his third glass.

'It's my fault,' Felipe said and tried to hold Agustina's hand.

'Of course it's your fault,' she spat and withdrew her hand.

'She was cold, wasn't she? I mean, we are sure, aren't we?' asked Leonel.

'Why did she come?' asked Felipe taking his glass.

'To look for me. To talk to me,' Agustina said. 'To tell me that you two were making up stories about her and God knows what other shit. That's why she came. To fuck with me.'

'Well, it worked, didn't it?' said Leonel and a trickle of whisky fell down his chin. 'We are all fucked.'

'Stop it, both of you,' I said and gave Leonel a napkin.

'She started it,' he said.

'No. He started it,' said Agustina, pointing to her father.

'What did she want?' insisted Felipe.

'Who cares, Dad?' said Leonel.

'I told you. She wanted to talk to me. She wanted to tell

me she couldn't believe she wasn't invited to the wedding. She said this was her house. When I got here she was looking at all those photographs on the dining-room table. She said that you two wanted to blame her for something she didn't do. She said you were a son of a bitch who –'

'Why don't you shut up?' said Leonel and he filled his glass again.

'He asked me,' said Agustina.

'Anything else?' asked Felipe and he took a cigarette from Leonel's pack. He hadn't smoked in twenty years and I almost said: don't.

'She also said that my mother forced her to have an abortion. Either she is stupid or she thinks I am. I was there that night when she asked you to help her find a clinic,' Agustina said.

'Why don't you all shut up?' said Leonel. 'Or let's talk about something else. How is Agustina's dress going, Mum?'

'Is that it?' asked Felipe.

'What do you want me to tell you, Dad?' Agustina shouted. 'Do you want me to lie and say she came looking for you?'

'Agustina, shut your fucking mouth,' said Leonel, his eyes closed, his hands over his ears.

'Is that what you want, old man? Comfort? Well, there is none. Not for you. Not for me. And it is all your fault,' said Agustina.

Leonel stood up and from the jacket that had been on his lap the dog bones fell to the floor.

'Let's go to bed,' he said, taking his time to collect all the bones.

'She didn't love you, Dad. She made fun of us all,' Agustina said. 'She made a fool out of you. And look at us now. Covered in grass and dirt.'

Leonel hit her on the shoulder and she jumped to her feet.

'Stop it!' I warned and they both froze. Then the weight of the night fell on them both, and I saw the fear on their faces. I sent them to bed and I heard Leonel ask Agustina, 'Can we sleep with you?' Then he whistled, the dogs ran upstairs behind them and the four of them locked themselves in Agustina's bedroom.

Someone is humming. It's not Agustina. We are alone. It must be me, then. My head feels heavy. This head that is not green or yellow. I can't see with my right eye. Or can I? I don't know which one is my right eye. If I touch it I feel it but I don't want to move my hand, this hand that is so heavy that I don't know if it is mine or if someone attached it to my body by mistake. I think I have a layer of mildew over my right eye. Why do I speak? To clear the mildew away. Does it go? I don't know. Is it gone, Agustina? Energy comes and goes. Maybe my brain has grown white and green filaments.

A young woman looks at me. Come. What is your name? Surprise. Fear. Disgust. What is your name? 'Agustina, Mum, Agustina,' she says. Just like my daughter. Agustina. What? Hey, sweetie, have you seen Rafael? He is very small and grey. Grey? Grey and pink. Agustina, you should return all the things you stole from our house guests. And those notebooks, really, what were you thinking? Look how dirty you are. Clean your shoes, fix your braids. Make sure someone feeds Tavo, I left some bean burritos on the counter. Don't cry, dear, I'm sure your mother will come and get you. Do cry, Agustina, cry now because you can, cry and shout. I don't want to cry. I don't feel like it. I am tired but I have done nothing all day. Did you confirm the tent? No one can see me. I think I have gone. If I go, will the mildew go as well? With light comes reality.

'Move, Mum. No, I won't take you to the tree.'

Take me to the tree, I want to see the sun rise.

'No.'

Take me Agustina. Be careful. No, I am fine, I swear I am fine, I just need some air. Outside. Take me to the tree. Thank you. Two men cover the sun with a canvas roof, what are they doing? A little to the right, yes. Shorter. Now they lay a wooden floor over the grass. The girl looks into my eyes, what a beautiful white dress she is wearing. Who made your dress, dear? She looks like a bride. You look like a bride, sweetie, are you getting married? She kisses me and the sun goes up. When did the sun go up? I thought it was morning already. Agustina, come here, help me close this zipper. What do you think, pearls or emeralds? You look so pale, did you sleep well? Are you nervous? You don't have to get married if you don't want to. It's not a big deal, it's just a green Constanza, that is all. I am in the garden. I am in Chihuahua. I am on the swing by the orchard, look how dirty you are. Who is in that box? No one told Tavo I was going away. Plants, the plants look at me, I hide behind the tree. The mildew grows when it reaches the leaves, green over green. Can you pass me the sewing kit? That table cloth is dirty. Look, there is Rafael! We've been looking everywhere for you, little one, why are you covered in dirt? It's raining like I knew it would. It's just a spot, just a tiny spot of mildew, nothing more. It's raining and the tent is ripped, remove all the table cloths! Rafael, you are filthy, get Leonel to give you a bath. It's not sick, it's dead but it doesn't know it. Dad, you must sit at this table, have Felipe walk you to it. Leonel, get some buckets to collect the rain. The grass will be ruined. Get those bones off that table, can't you see your sister is getting married? Out, damned spot, out I say! It's nothing, I am just tired. I am fine. A trunk. A branch. Agustina, is that you? Look, Constanza just got here.

CB *editions*

Founded in 2007, CB editions publishes chiefly short fiction (including work by Will Eaves, Gabriel Josipovici, David Markson and May-Lan Tan) and poetry (Andrew Elliott, Beverley Bie Brahic, Nancy Gaffield, J. O. Morgan, D. Nurkse). Writers published in translation include Apollinaire, Andrzej Bursa, Joaquín Giannuzzi, Gert Hofmann, Agota Kristof and Francis Ponge.

Books can be ordered from www.cbeditions.com.